SAGEBRUSH JUSTICE

Barbara Schmidt

Auctorem House
276 5th Ave, Ste 704-2591
New York, NY 10001
www.auctoremhouse.com
1.888.332.7718

CONTENTS

This book is dedicated to all those
Who read it and encouraged me
While trying to have it printed.
To my daughter Kimberly
And all my other friends.

Initially inspired by the song "If You Could Read My Mind" by Gordon Lightfoot.

Other story ideas taken from:

- Laura Ingalls Wilder's books
- World Atlas Encyclopedias
- Song "Gypsys, Tramps & Thieves" by Cher
- Plus many other books too numerous to mention

My own personal experiences and my own mind.

INTRODUCTION

Before the war between the states, those who traveled west were mainly those who wanted a better life for themselves and their families. After the war, many of those who went west were gold seekers, trying to get rich quick, and some who had to get their families out of where they lived for one reason or another.

This is the story of one family that fell into the latter category. The events may or may not have happened. The towns did exist at that time, and some of them exist to this day. Also included in this story are Ned Buntline, George Armstrong Custer, the Little Bighorn, Buffalo Bill Cody, Chicago World's Fair and other fairs, Annie Oakley, Queen Victoria and other kings and queens of Europe, the car, and the telephone. For more information on these and all the cities, states, and countries listed in this story, consult your local library, an encyclopedia, or even your internet.

THE JOURNEY

HE WAGON TRAIN stretches out twenty-five wagons strong. They are pulled by horses, mules, and oxen. The teams of horses and mules are driven by the boys, sixteen to eighteen years of age. The oxen are goaded by the boys, fourteen to sixteen years of age. Of course, many of the men are also driving the teams. Those with riding horses allow them to be ridden by anybody who can ride so that they can herd the cattle and the extra horses and mules.

The sick, the elderly, and the very young are the only ones who can ride in the wagons. All of the wagons are used for sleeping, except five, and they carry water and other supplies for the journey. Almost everyone in the train is related by blood, marriage, or both. There are a few that are just very close friends.

My name is Rebecca Sage, but most people call me Becky, and my husband's name is Oden.

When we left our homes, it was December 8, 1868. The snow were still on the ground in most areas, which made it slow traveling. The streams and small rivers were still frozen over and that made it easy to cross the waterways. Yesterday, January 30, 1869, we had crossed one of those many rivers. It was early evening when we crossed her, so we decided to camp right there once everyone was across. While we lay in our beds, we heard some strange noises.

Some of the men went out and looked around. When they returned later, they told us that it was the ice on the river breaking up. We made across at the right time; in another day, we would have to cross further on down river.

Many carpetbaggers had come in after the war, taking advantage of those who would not or could not pay their back taxes, or those who did not return home after the war in time to take charge of their places. For four years, we tried to make a go of it, but finally we realized we couldn't do it. It is with deep regrets that we decided to go west. For six years we watched as things changed, and we knew war was coming. In preparation, we had started saving up the northern currency; as a result, we were able to save enough to pay ten years' worth of back taxes. And we wanted to have some money so that if the South won the war and we wanted to visit the North, we would have spending money. But if the North won, we would have to pay the back taxes because we did not want to lose our lands.

When the carpetbaggers came in, they said that they would accept a partial payment of at least one-third of what was owed. We said that they could borrow the money so that they would not lose their land either, and they could pay us back when they got on their feet. We even said that we would not charge any interest. All but one of the families would not hear of it saying that we were traitors. The one family that accepted our offer ended up going with us because they too became outcasts. That is when our neighbors burned down the main house. The house had been used as a field hospital, so it had been spared the ravages of war.

At first, it was just my husband and I who wanted to go west. When we made the announcement, the other family members tried to talk us out of leaving, but as the weeks just prior to our leaving passed, other members of our families decided to join us until all were going west. This included both sets of grandparents and parents, brothers and sisters, and all of the children of both my husband and myself.

*   *   *

One of my brothers is a lawyer, and his name is Mark. He will remain behind to make sure we get a fair deal for everyone's land. He will be joining us just as soon as we let him know where we are.

All of the married couples will sleep in their own wagons; the single women and older girls will sleep two or three to a wagon according to age. The children sleep four or five to a wagon according to age and sex. The single men and older boys will also sleep two or three to a wagon until the weather warms up. After that, they will sleep on the ground around or under the wagons.

In these first months of travel, the breakfasts have consisted of warm, jerked beef, eggs, and biscuits. They are served bright and early in the morning, before the sun comes. They are hurried because we wish to be off as the sun is rising in the east. Lunch is cold beans, corn bread, or biscuits that were made the night before. It too is a hurry-up meal so that we can cover as much ground as possible in one day. The evening meal consists of some of the wild game that can be found in the area of the campsite. It is slow because we are no longer in a hurry. We can eat as much as we want to. And this is also the time we prepare the breads for the next day's breakfast and lunch.

In the long hours of travel, if there are any wild fruits, nuts, or berries to be found along the way, the older boys and girls pick as many of them as possible so that the younger children would not complain of being hungry during the day. Of course, they make sure that they stay close to the wagon train so that they won't get lost.

Almost every night, the ones who can play an instrument do so while others sing and dance. That is, everyone who is able to participate does so. Those unable to take part sit and knit things for others. There will be two babies born soon; one is my brother Aaron's fourth child and the other is my first. Every so often, other families or even individuals join the train and travel with us, and while they are with us, they take part in the festivities. Then after a few days go by, they travel on in their own direction. Some of them go southwest, but most of them go northwest to Oregon.

Each night, while traveling, the men and older boys take turns hunting. They go out in groups of no less than five, looking for wild game. Others cut and bring in firewood for the fires, and they feed and water the livestock. Some of them bring in water to fill up the water barrels. The younger boys pick up any buffalo chips that they find around the campsite. Our guides had told us that once they are dry, they burn as good and sometimes better than and longer than wood. The women and girls prepare the food to be cooked, which includes the bread for the next day. The children too young to help can play around the campsite. Everyone has to help in some way, whether it is at their own wagon or with someone else. Before each meal, a different person carries the fire bucket around to each fire site within the circle. So far it has taken us two weeks to go across Missouri. We enter Tennessee somewhere between the North Carolina state line and Chattanooga, Tennessee. Then we cross to where Arkansas, Missouri, and Tennessee all intersect.

June 5, 1869

Last night's stop was our last before leaving Missouri. We were a few miles northwest of Joplin when one of my nephews got too close to the edge of the river where we camped, and he fell in. He was born with defect in one leg, which made it difficult for him to swim in deep water, but he could swim a little in shallow water. Before anyone could get to him, he drowned. Early this morning, we buried his body and spent about two more hours there to mourn his passing. His father had died in the war, then his mother died three years ago. Now the oldest brother was looking after all of the children. After two hours there, we moved on to find our home. We made camp at seven o'clock tonight.

Sunday, June 25, 1869

We have not traveled at all today because it is the day we worship the Lord our Creator. The food was not cooked today, so we eat only cold foods; everything was fixed last night. Our meats are dried, or we don't eat any meat at all.

Because all preparations of today were done last night, we had to stop the wagons early enough to get all the things done before it got too dark. All the chores which could not wait until Monday were done today. Among the things that had to be done today was milking the cows, otherwise we would not get as much milk until they calved again. Feeding and watering the animals was another job that had to be done. Just like us, they too had to eat.

The seating arrangement was put up last night too. When it was cold, the chairs and benches had been put up around a center fire. Now that it was warmer, the center fire is no longer needed, but the seating is still in the middle. This morning, like all Sunday mornings, we worship God by singing songs such as "Come Thou Almighty King," "Come Thou Fount," "Come We That Love the Lord," "There is a Fountain," and many others. With all that and prayers, it took all morning. The early afternoon was spent hearing a message given to us by my brother Aaron who is an ordained minister. For the rest of the afternoon and into the evening, all we do is rest. Not even the children can play their games. From sunup to sundown on Sunday, this is our schedule during the trip. Once we find our land and settle down, the central location for worship will be a building.

July 7, 1869

Yesterday afternoon while we were traveling, one young girl named Kimberly became sick, but it wasn't until we stopped for the night that everyone realized just how sick she was. All through the night, her parents took turns staying up with her, keeping her cool until her fever broke, which didn't happen until late afternoon. Because of the hour and Kim still being weak, we decided to stay here for one more day.

July 8, 1869

It was a good thing that we decided to stay one more night because last night just after the evening meal, five more children became sick with the same thing. Their parents stayed up with them also, keeping them cool. Earlier today, eight more children became ill, which gave Andrew, who is a doctor, a fit about what was causing the children to get sick. After each child was better, Andrew would ask them what they had eaten or drank the day before. Since none of the children had eaten or drank anything different than anyone else did, Andrew was so puzzled he told us he thinks that we should move on a half a day to see if that is it.

At the same time, he sent one of the young adults north to a town that we had heard about to bring back their doctor. When they got in, the doctor looked at the sick children, and they pooled their knowledge. They decided that the children had eaten something different, only it was three days earlier, on the fourth. And it took some of them longer to get sick because their system was stronger. Other children either had just a mild stomachache or nothing at all because their system was strong enough to throw the poison off.

Once it was cleared up as what the problem was and the children were better, we were able to move on. That was a good sign because not one of the children who got sick died. We count that a blessing from God. That, along with the fact that there was a doctor in a nearby town that could help out.

July 10, 1869

It is two days after the children got sick. This afternoon, when passing through a small valley, we saw the results of where a tornado had gone through and realized that the Lord had allowed the children to get sick because he knew if they had not gotten sick, then we would have been right in the path of the tornado when it hit.

Now in Kansas, we start looking for a place to settle down. Since we want a good place to call our own, a place where we can grow good crops and strong children, we take more time to eat the noon meal, and we stop earlier in the day to give the men more time to look around the area. We also move slower and take more rest stops during the day for that very purpose.

July 20, 1869

Late this afternoon, while the wagon train was traveling along, one of my husband's nieces got directly in front of one of the team of horses. It would have been all right except that a snake scared the team and they bolted forward, trampling her underfoot. As a result, a rule was made that no one is to walk directly in front of the teams to prevent that from happening again. We will remain here the rest of the day while we bury her body and allow her parents and siblings a time to grieve.

August 6, 1869

This morning, we buried my husband's great-grandfather. He had been ill for the last two weeks. He was hoping to see our new homes before he died, but he didn't make it. We will spend the rest of this morning here, then move on after lunch. We all loved him very much, and we'll miss him very much. He was the oldest member of our group and was a fine example for everyone to follow. Now his widow is the oldest.

August 15, 1869

Today is my nineteenth birthday. We have been on the move every day now since the first part of December 1868. I did not expect any gifts, let alone a party, but I got both. My husband kept me away from my father's wagon until after supper. Although I did suspect something was going on, I could not even guess what it was. At that time, he took me to the biggest party this side of the Rockies. Again, there are some visitors that had been traveling with us. They have been with us for the last two days and are due to leave us sometime tomorrow afternoon. The party was terrific; I got both store-bought and handmade gifts. Even the visitors gave me a little something, though it wasn't much. The party was given at night, just like all the other times that there was a birthday celebrated on the trail, but at those times not everyone on the two sides came, and sometimes there were no visitors with us.

Day after day, we go deeper into Kansas. Every day we hope that maybe today, maybe on this stop, maybe this time, we wouldn't have to move on. This is now the last week in August. It has been slow travel, and we are unable to find a suitable place to settle down, so we travel on into the Colorado territory. Kansas wasn't to be our new home.

August 30, 1869

While we were preparing our morning meal, a group of men rode up and asked us what we were doing there. We told them that we had just stopped there overnight and that we were going to move on just as soon as we finished eating and that we knew it was privately owned. The man in charge told us that the land from here a day's journey on west is held in partnership by all the ranchers around here. They had filed on the land several years ago so that they could have a place to graze their cattle.

We had invited the men to stay for breakfast, and they accepted. It was during the meal that my husband told them that they should let in a few farmers so that the ranchers could have winter crops for their dinner plates and maybe convince some of them to raise grain for the cattle. The leader said that they would like to let in a few farmers, they had discussed it with the other ranchers, and when one or two would come through, they would be invited to settle down in this valley. They even asked if one or two of us would like to stay on. The offer was discussed during breakfast, but everyone turned it down.

The boss sent two of his men back to his place where he has a few apple trees and had them bring back a few bags of apples and gave them to us. Those same two men are to accompany us to the edge of the property line so that the other ranchers in the partnership would know that we are just passing through and not stopping.

THE SETTLEMENT

September 9, 1869

TODAY IS THURSDAY. For the first six and a half days of travel into the Colorado territory, we have more of the same bad luck in finding a home. So we continue on searching for our home. When we stop for the noon meal today, the men come back with a good report, and the guides come back with fresh meat and the report that there is plenty of wild game in the area. So we decide that this is where we will settle down. It's about time too because the small children are growing travel weary; needless to say, the rest are a bit tired. Our tempers are even shorter than our meat, which is very low.

While looking for game in the area, our guides also look for markers that will tell people that the land is claimed and to put up ours if they find none to let others know that the land is now claimed. When they return, they report that they have found no markers for hundreds of miles, but they do find a small band of Indians and make a trade agreement with them in our behalf, which will benefit both parties. The Indians will bring us game and other things, and we will give them part of our potatoes or other things.

And so we send the two guides on to the nearest town, which is Silverton. It is a small mining town four days' journey farther west and a little north of where we stopped. They go to register our claims so that no one can come along later and take our lands away from us after we have worked so hard to develop the land. They also take letters along with them to be mailed so that those we left behind will know where to come to, and they will buy us some more supplies and bring them back to us. Since we have about two and a half weeks' worth of supplies, we gave them permission to stay on in Silverton for about a week before heading to us. We know that we can trust them to do it because about two months after we hired them to guide us, they made professions of faith in God, and their time with us showed that they did get saved.

All we have to do is live here for five years and work the land, but if one man gives up before the five years are up, then he and his family loses his section of land. No one else in the family can get his land; it goes back to the government for others to live. If someone else does come in to live on the land that one of us had first, we will not hold that against them. In fact, we will welcome them into the area. They aren't to blame for the people losing the land. The only way that the family can hang onto the land is if someone is buried there before the five years are up, then the land goes to the nearest of kin automatically. Of course, we are all hoping that we won't have to do that for many years to come.

September 11, 1869

This morning, in honor of the settlement, Aaron performed the first wedding in nine months. My first cousin James and my husband's second cousin LeeAnn were wed this afternoon. James' first wife died in childbirth, and LeeAnn's husband died in the war, a few months later she gave birth to a girl. It was a happy time for us all here today. During the reception, Joseph Moore, a fourth cousin on both sides, announced that he would marry my girlfriend Jill exactly one year from the day we found this land, thus bringing her into this family officially.

September 15, 1869

Today is the fourth day of our encampment. After the cleanup of the noon meal is finished, the men continue to make plans, as they have done for the past three days. They decide where each man's house and outbuildings are to be built, who will work on the different houses, and when they will be worked on. The houses will be built first than the outbuildings. At this time, they have finished the plans for about one-fourth of the sites. I had gone across the camp to visit with my brother's wife. After talking to her for a while, I head back to my own wagon because it is time to feed my daughter. After I get done feeding, I will need to go over to my sister-in-law's wagon to talk to her about her daughter's birthday party. I will need to talk to her again later to finalize the plans.

Along with the plans for the houses and other buildings, one of the buildings they plan for is a church, and with that, some of the men are starting to set up the chairs for Sunday services and the women fix the foods that will be eaten tomorrow.

September 16, 1869

Today is Sunday. Once again this morning, we sat and worshipped the Lord as we always do, and like always, the only chores done today were those that had to be done. Not even the men made plans for the rest of the buildings. That job, the planning and the building, will have to wait until Monday morning.

September 17, 1869

Monday morning, the men are getting back to making the plans for each building, where they will be, and who will build each one. And some of them will build a large barn close by for the supplies until we have our own places up.

September 18, 1869

Today is Tuesday. Early this morning, about a dozen men go out to one of the selected sites and start building one of the houses. About a dozen more went to another site also; they will continue until all of the houses are built. Once the houses are finished, then they will start on the barns. The women prepare an extra big lunch and take it to where the men are working. Dinner is lighter but ready when the men return at night.

THE ATTACK

THIS MORNING, JUST after breakfast, while I was talking to Connie about her grandmother's birthday party tonight and before the men had a chance to leave to work on the houses, five men came into the camp to get something to eat, and being the kind of people that we are, they were fed. After feeding Amy her breakfast, I headed for my sister's wagon to talk to her. When I reached the center of the circle, disaster hit. The men had told us that they were cattlemen up from New Mexico territory on a buying trip. They actually came into camp to spy us out. They had set up a prearranged signal with the rest of their men. These men wanted to find out how many guns we have and how much stuff we have and would it be worth robbing us.

When they found out what they wanted to know, they fired off a shot. We couldn't figure out what they were doing until the rest of their band came from behind a small rise about five hundred yards to the west, taking us completely by surprise. The men who were to go out and work on the buildings didn't even have a chance to go out. They shot every one of us, starting with those with guns on so that we could not defend the others and ending with those of us who could not even defend themselves at all. And since I was sort of a tomboy, I too wore a gun, and I was among those first to be shot.

Three bullets hit me. The first one went into my right leg just above the knee, causing me to go down on my knees. Just as I started to rise, the second one got me in the left shoulder, knocking me back down. The third bullet took a small chunk out of my left side as I was starting rise again, knocking me completely down and into unconsciousness. They continued to shoot the rest of my people, from the oldest and ending with the youngest child that they could see.

Because the three bullets came at me rather fast, I never had a chance to draw my gun; it was still in the holster when the third bullet knocked me down. Because we were not able to defend ourselves, every man, woman, and child is dead or dying, except for the two babies. In about a half hour all was quiet—all except for the men moving the stuff around in the wagons. In the process, they discovered the two babies that are four and five weeks old, but they refuse to take them along with them because they're extra baggage. When they finished, they took the wagons with our belongings, which turned out to be ten, and headed south. They also took along all of our stock, except for one horse that was badly wounded. Another horse was killed during the shooting. Several of the children had dogs as pets, and some of the men had hunting dogs. Any dog that would not accept the new men as masters were killed.

Before the attack began, I saw the faces of two of the five men who came into the camp, and during the attack, I saw three of the men who did the shooting. After the attack, I saw the face of the man as he took my gun as I was conscious when the man bent down to take it, and he saw that. Why he didn't shoot me again I didn't know; I guess he didn't think I could survive with a bullet in my side. What I didn't know at the time, nor did he, is that the bullet didn't enter my body. Because of the wound in my side and the process of him removing my gun, the pain became so bad that I passed out again. While I was conscious this time, I saw more of the men as they moved around the campsite.

It was at this time that I saw one of the first two men whom I had seen earlier, and he was now giving orders to the others; my guess was that he was the boss. I was sure that if I could survive, I could find a way to take revenge, be it with or without a badge. I hoped someone else would survive because they could help me hunt them down. I must survive! I must—I must!

The third time I regained consciousness, I saw no one and heard no noises. The attackers were gone, but to where I didn't know. During this time of being conscious, I believe that there were some more of my people still alive. I didn't know who or where they were or how many. I just had a feeling that there were others.

September 21, 1869

This is the fourth time I regained consciousness, and this time, there are men in the campsite but not as many this time. They are all moving around the campsite, some carrying the bodies of my family, while others are carrying shovels. Still others have brought water and bandages into the center where I am lying. They have set up a shelter here and brought all the wounded and placed them beside me. There seems to be about twenty men, and they are doing whatever there is needed to be done for my family.

One of the men here has a nanny goat so that he can drink her milk every day; he has a bad stomach. None of the men here ever makes fun of him because he has been with them for a long time, and he has had this trouble for a short time. On top of that, he is a much bigger and stronger man than most of them, and he can outfight, outshoot, and outride any five of them put together. He is giving all of us some of the milk so that we can build up our strength before we are put into a wagon for the trip to the doctor for more treatment.

When I regain consciousness this time, I have noticed that they seem to be different. Their dress and manners seem different to me, something I have seen before. The man taking care of me tells me that they are buffalo hunters and that they are following a small herd of them when they see the buzzards circling above. He also tells me that he is in charge of these men and the date. He says that they found us late last night, just before dark. He tells me that there are a total of seven other adults and one child, a boy, still alive, besides the two babies, that is five men and two other women with me. It will be a miracle if the other adults survive. He says it is a miracle that I was not hit any worse. If these men have not come along when they did, I might not have survived either.

I have noticed that the men have buried the two horses and all the dogs in the area where the two horses had died. I think that, that is a good idea; it is a good way to keep the wolves and vultures from eating the flesh and spoiling the area. They bury my family members on the complete opposite side of the campsite.

September 23, 1869

After two hard days of work, they had finished burying the dead, and they put the wounded into a wagon. One of the two women, the boy, and two of the men died before we left, and they were buried while we were still at the campsite. They wished to get us to the nearest town where we could get medical care, so they hitched their horses to a wagon and headed to Silverton. In the meantime, several of the men took most of the horses on so that there would be fresh horses along the way. Those men had started out the morning after they found us, leaving behind six horses at each meal stop until they got near the town. One man went on into town to let the doctor and the sheriff know what is going on.

They did that so that when the wagon got to them, they would have fresh horses to hitch to the wagon. They traveled day and night, stopping only long enough to change the tired horses to fresh ones. The tired horses would be brought up later after they had rested. When they put us in the wagon, along with myself and the two babies, among those who were still alive was my husband Oden, my brother Jim, my brother-in-law David, and a cousin.

Going day and night, the time for the trip was cut from four and a half days down to two and a half days. My brother and brother-in-law died on the way in. Jim died on the evening of the first day, and David died an hour before they arrived in town. The men did not wish to take the time to bury them even though they had time to take the bodies out when they changed horses. Instead, they brought them on into town to be buried there. They wanted to try to save my husband's and cousin's lives.

September 25, 1869

They arrived with us at midmorning on the third day. The doctor immediately took us up to his office for medical care. We would be in his office for a few days. That afternoon, the people buried my brother and brother-in-law in the town cemetery so that they could have a final resting place. The doctor had commented on how well the men had dressed our wounds. That night, my cousin died, and the next morning, she was buried beside the others.

On the afternoon of the day, they arrived in town with us, our guides brought the money to the sheriff and told him of their part in the party and what the money was originally to be used for. They had heard from the buffalo hunters about the massacre. They were just getting ready to make their purchases for us, but they decided to wait until the men got us into town to see if it was the party they were leading. If it was their party, they were going to do the right thing and turn the money in. They felt that the money should go to the survivors for their care.

The guides said that there was another brother who should be on his way out here by now, and he could take care of us when he and his family would get here. They said that it was their understanding that he was a lawyer, but they were not sure. They also told the sheriff that they had registered the claims for the lands where we had set up camp.

RECOVERY

October 4, 1869

TWO DAYS AFTER we arrived in town, my husband and I were moved over to the hotel where there was more room for us. Of all those who were still alive when the men found us, none of them ever regained consciousness except my husband and I. My husband regained consciousness three days before he died; as a result, the doctor thought we were both to make it. Everyone else thought he was going to make it too. Ten days after we got into town, he took a turn for the worse and died. He too was buried in the town cemetery. For three days after the attack, I was in and out of consciousness. After that, I started regaining my strength. While still in bed, I told everyone who each family member was, when and where each was born, all that took place the last nine months, and the date of the attack.

The guides and the buffalo hunters gave them the information about the site so that it can be found again. The hunters also gave the sheriff photos of those who lived beyond the day of the attack for future use. The buffalo hunters left town three days after they brought us into town. They can tolerate a big town only for so long before they have to leave even though Silverton isn't all that big.

December 3, 1869

Last night, I went to a Friday night barn dance with the doctor, his wife, and their son who is about my age. There was another young man there named Robert who was just a few years older than me, and every time the music would start up, he would ask me to dance with him. Even though I did dance with him a few times, I couldn't do it all the time. It wouldn't be fair to the other men or even the young man I came with. I did dance with some of the others, but I couldn't dance with everyone as I had to sit some of them out so that I wouldn't get too tired. When we left the dance, Robert asked me if he could pick me up for church Sunday morning, and as he was the first to ask, I agreed. I had to turn everyone else down who asked because Robert beat them to it.

December 4, 1869

This morning, Robert came and picked me up for church. I had attended services there before, and I had met him there, but he didn't really get to know me until the barn dance. Afterward we went out to a church picnic, then back to the hotel. We sat in the lobby and talked for a while, then he left, and I went upstairs.

December 11, 1869

One week later. This morning, Robert picked me for church again. Afterward we went to the restaurant for lunch. We talked again for a while. We had been seeing each other during the week, and when he left, he hinted that he wanted to marry me, but it was only a hint, and it was too early for me to remarry.

December 22, 1869

Even though I had been talking for some time about going out and hunting the men down, Robert still proposed to me. He said that he loved me and wanted me to stay with him for the rest of my life, or his, whichever comes first. I told him it was a lovely thought, but it was too early for me to remarry, and I couldn't settle down knowing that those men were walking around free and alive. But we could still be good friends and keep seeing each other when I am in town.

February 15, 1870

I am fully recovered from my wounds now, and the doctor has released me from his care, but I am to hang around for a while because some of the townspeople want to fix a memorial for my family so that all who see it will know what happened out there.

Our former guides led a small delegation of people from the town out to the burial site, and I went with them. We took the bodies of my family with us so that they could be buried beside the others. The townspeople put a fence up to keep animals off the graves, leaving one corner for the three surviving members. Other family members would have to be buried outside the fence but within another fenced in area, which was large enough for several dozens of graves.

Then a plaque was put up at the entrance of the place; it told who is buried there, when and where each was born, and the date of the attack. It also told why we came west, who found us, and when. They also put down the two babies' names and my own as the only survivors of the attack. After the fences were put up, there was still some lumber leftover, enough so that they were able to add a fence around the area where the horses and dogs were buried so that the human burial site would not go into that area, and it was marked as the animal grave site.

There were a total of ninety-five killed that day. Ninety-eight left Georgia, two were born on the trail, and three died on the trail. There were ninety-two family members and five members of another family living on the day of the attack. These were the only people on the train that day. Although there were others earlier that week, except for the spies, there were no others.

While I was recovering, a woman my age named Katherina was constantly with me. She became my nurse, caring for me. She also took care of my daughter and nephew until my brother and his family could get here. After my brother got here, she continued to care for me. Some of her family were killed by Indians. While the Indians were attacking, the solders came and killed many of the Indians and took the rest of them prisoner. That action had saved much of her family.

Also, while I was recovering, I talked to a circuit judge about getting an execution order for the men so that I can hunt them down and imprison or kill the men who were involved in the attack that day. The judge told me that he would think it over for a while and let me know when I feel better. I want the judge to get papers from someone in Washington to make me a marshal with a badge. If they do give me a badge, I will send as many of them to jail and the gallows as I possibly can. When I find the man who gave the orders to kill, I will shoot him like he had his men do to us. But not until after I get as many names from him as I can. I may even let him believe that he will go on trial if he does give me names. The others, including the other four, I don't know yet if I will kill them. I will decide that at the time.

February 20, 1870

It has been five days since the doctor released me from his care. This afternoon the judge told me that he was able to get me a marshal's badge and an execution order for all the men that I saw. He said that I would be able to shoot the men if I wanted, and it would be legal. I will hunt them down, every one of them, especially the five. It will be unusual for a woman to wear a marshal's badge, even though there are a few that are sheriffs. But I am the only adult survivor of the attack and the only one who can do it. Plus, they must be punished. This evening Katherina told me that she wants to go with me and help me in any way she can.

February 25, 1870

Tonight I saw Robert for the last time. He took me out to dinner and a moonlight walk. I told him that I was leaving the next morning on the manhunt. He knew to try and talk me out of the hunt was a waste of time, so he didn't even try. He did say that he would always love me, and he would wait for me as long as he could, but if he found someone else and fell in love with her, he would marry her. I knew it was best for him, and I told him so, for I did not know how long the hunt would last.

THE HUNT

February 26, 1870

THIS MORNING, THE judge swore me as a marshal and Kate as deputy and gave me a few extra badges in case we brought someone else in to join the hunt for a while. So that was how we started our journey. The judge had told me that I could kill them all without questions; the warrant I had gave me that right. The one man who I really want to kill is the one I saw in our camp that afternoon, the one who gave the orders. The others will go to jail, unless they force my hand, and I have to kill them.

All my expenses will be paid for through a special fund that was set up after our guides turned our money over to the sheriff, and that account is in Silverton. I can just cable him, and he will cable the money back, whatever amount I ask for. I have decided that before I kill the leader, I will find out why they killed everyone in my family, instead of just robbing us and leaving us out without food and water to die. I will also get as many names as he can give me.

April 10, 1870

We arrived in Liberty, Colorado, the town where Kate's mother lives. Kate wanted to tell her mother what happened to me and that we will be traveling together for a while. She wanted her mother to know what we were doing so that if she doesn't hear from her for a spell, she won't get worried. We were going to stay here for a few days, so we decided that while we here, I would check around to see if there were any of the men around who was involved in the attack. But we found none, although there were rumors there were some south of here down toward Texas.

July 14, 1870

While passing through a small town in Southcentral Texas (we had stopped here last night to take a two-day break) we had gone to see the sheriff last night and told him our story. This morning, while walking around town with one of the deputies, a man passed out as we approached him. Later in the doctor's office, he told the sheriff why he collapsed. It was because he was one of the men who took our stuff from us. He came along in the attack because he was a habitual gambler. He had lost all of the stuff he had taken from us and had no idea where any of it was. Once the men had divided our stuff, they went their own separate ways, and he lost track of them. He gave me twenty names, but he did not know where they could be now. He also told us that there was between a hundred and fifty to two hundred men. He couldn't remember how many because he was also a drunk. He was tried and convicted of robbery and murder and sentenced to life in prison with no chance of parole because of his state of mind.

November 1, 1870

A little over ten and a half months of searching have now passed since we started out. I finally came across the first of the five men that I had seen that day. Other than God directing my path, I did not think it would be this soon. I had figured that it would take over a year. When he spotted me, he turned as white as a ghost because he thought he was seeing a ghost. He thought all were dead, including me. Between the one in July and this one, I had found two more of the men. And the same fate happened to them as the first man.

I tried to get his gun and get his name and the names of his partners. He refused to cooperate and ran for it. I fired one shot into the air, and he turned and fired at me, at which time I shot him. The sheriff heard the shots and came running with his gun out. I knew the shots would bring him running, so I had put my gun away and got my badge and papers out by the time he got to me. After he saw the badge, he put away his gun and read the papers. He saw that the papers said that if I found any of the five men I could recognize, I could shoot them if I want. I also told the sheriff that I did not want to shoot him until I got names, but he gave me no out.

While I was in the sheriff's office, telling him what happened to me a year ago and the shooting today, one of his deputies came in to see if he could be of any help. It turned out that he was one of the men involved in the attack, but I didn't know it. He had seen me while I was unconscious. In fact, he had my gun and holster. He had bought them from the man who had taken them from me because he wanted to drink and drown the memory of that day. But try as he could, the memory of seeing all those children shot down without a chance to grow up just would not leave him alone. The deputy told us that the man had said that he didn't think that it would bother him, but as the weeks turned into months, he had more and more nightmares about that day. He also said that the man died in his drunken stupor. That left only three more of the men of whom I had seen. The sheriff locked him up and was charged with murder. The reason that he had the deputy job only a year after the attack was that he was from here.

Before the trial, I got many more names from the former deputy, but he could not give me all the names other than first names or a nickname as he did not know all of them. He also said some were from England, Mexico, Canada, and a few other European countries. After the trial, I got back my families' things that he had, including my gun and holster. I now have two guns; one will be kept in my saddle bag in case of an emergency. It was then that I found out that there were two hundred men involved in the attack on my family. That made four men dead so far, one I killed, one killed himself, one went to jail for the rest of his life, but he died there, and the last one was hung.

From what the deputy told me, I now know my journey will continue for many years to come. The length of time is not yet known. At the time I got the warrant, I did not know how many there were. There was no number, it just said, "All of the men responsible for the attack, as listed on separate sheets." I didn't know how many men there were until the deputy told me. I intend that every time that I find a man on the list, I would show it to him so that he can add or subtract names, if he was so inclined to do so.

I intend that whenever I would come to a city or town, I would go immediately to the local law officials. I would show them my badge and papers to see if there is someone living there under those or similar names. Whether there is or not, I would hang around there for a few days to see what the reaction of the citizens of the town would be when they see me. One or two deputies would be requested to stay with me while in the town. He would see the reaction of each man, and they would help me take him to jail, but only if he showed any fear when he saw me. Only the guilty need fear me.

August 1, 1871

Eighteen months have passed since we started out. This morning, we had stopped at a stage stop to get us a bit to eat and rest a few hours when a man came in to do the same thing. I had my back to the door, so he didn't see me at first. When I turned around, he saw me and tried to kill me, but I beat him to the draw. He was one of the men who came into the camp before the attack. In fact, he was the leader. I knew that he was because I heard him give the orders. I never got a chance to get any names from him because I killed him. Even though it was self-defense, the man that ran the station wanted to hold me for the marshal until I showed him my badge and papers.

December 1, 1871

Today I followed a man into Fayetteville, North Carolina, a small thriving town that is destined to go far. A town that lies on the Cape Fear River and was named for General Lafayette of France. He had fought with us and for us during our revolutionary war. When I got there, I found out that the man that I was after had gone to the sheriff. He had told the sheriff that there was someone following him, that he was a law-abiding citizen, and he wanted the protection of the law. I had gone to the sheriff as always, and when he saw me for the first time since the shooting, he fainted. He did not know that I was the one following him. When he came around, he confessed to being involved with the shooting. To him and the others, my wounds looked so bad that they thought that I too would die, otherwise they would have put another bullet into me. I would have died anyway were it not for the buffalo hunters; they came along at just the right moment. Another day and I would have died too, leaving only the two infants.

Since he was already in the sheriff's office, I asked that he be locked up. He could not give me any more names than I already had. He did confirm the fact that there were two hundred men, of which he only knew a few dozen names, and I already had them. After the trial, I got back all of our belongings that he still had. All of his things went to his family; I did not want anything that wasn't ours.

May 1, 1872

Last week, I followed one man to Boston. Upon seeing me, he fell from a third-floor window. I was out on the street, talking to a policeman. He had leaned out to get a better look at me, and when he realized who I was, he drew his gun to fire at me but lost his balance and fell. The judge there called it an accident and said I could have my things back if he had any of my things. While there, we would stay on until the first of June. We needed to rest for a while. I had heard a lot about this town and would like to see it.

By the first week in July, I was in New York. I had followed a man there, and he too fell to his death. This man and the one in Boston had gone there to inherit some money and property when he fell. In each of the two towns, the high society ladies asked me to join their clubs. When I was there, I dressed in fancy clothes, and because of that, they thought I was their kind of woman. I told them, no, thank you, because I had something to do. I would not tell them what I was doing; they never even guessed that I carried a badge. I wonder what they would have done had they found out about the badge.

When I left New York, it was late July 1872. I had heard about some of the men going down to Florida, to the Everglades, so I went down there. There I found out that there were three men there and that they had teamed up with four other men to do some gator hunting as alligator skin was becoming popular for shoes.

I was only able to get two of them because while I was in town looking for them, one of them fell out of the boat early in the day and an alligator got him. Unfortunately, one of the other men also was killed later that same day. I told the other three men about the attack on my family three years ago and showed them the badge and papers. Each of them gave me their blessing and told me that they would explain to the other man's family just how he died. The two men that I took prisoner here had given me the last of the two hundred men's names.

After three years of searching, I started finding myself back in Silverton. The people who were there when I was recovering from the wounds I had received knew that if they were to see me back in the area, it was for one of two reasons—either I was here to see my daughter and the rest of my family or I had followed the trail of one or more of the men who were responsible for the deaths of my family. Those who came to live there after I left on my search had heard of me from the others in town. They had seen the paintings that were done of me while I was recovering, and they recognized me from the paintings.

I have decided that whenever I returned, I will allow another painting to be done of me. Maybe later on, I will also pose for several statues to be done of me, maybe some on horseback and some on foot. Some full body and others bust, also some table size and others life-size.

February 14, 1873

Earlier today while riding on a stagecoach, five masked men stopped the stage. I was wearing a fancy eastern dress, an outfit I sometimes wear while traveling by stage or train, so they didn't pay too much attention to me other than I was a woman. One of the men was taking the handbags, wallets, and jewelry from us. When he got my handbag, he felt the badge. He took it out and looked at it, then he showed another man. That man said only two kinds of women carry a badge. One is the widow of a lawman. In that case the townspeople would get together and vote to give the badge that her husband wore to her with her husband's name engraved on the back.

The other case, the woman was a lawman herself, and if she was a lawman, then there was probably only one that I could be, and the papers inside my handbag would prove which one I was. He took out the papers and read them. Then after reading them for several minutes, he looked up at one of his men, then back down at the papers again. Then he took his gun from his holster and shot the man whom he had looked up at in the shoulder. He was told to get on the stage after his hands were bound. They then tied his horse to the back of the stage. That man was nervous from the moment I got out of the stage because he had recognized me, and he was afraid that I might recognize him. The leader told me to take the reward money for myself, and I was handed a wanted poster with his name and picture on it. He told me that he hated those who knowingly kill women and children, even if some of them were wearing guns, they were the mothers and grandmothers of our nation.

The man's name was then crossed off my list so that I would not go after him when he was already in jail. After that, he ordered that my things and the other passengers' things be returned to us. Everyone else on the stage benefited from my being on the stage today. I decided to keep the horse and money because I would need them when I got to my destination. As it turned out, his horse was actually one of ours. I knew that because of the brand—it was our brand, mine and my husband's. I would keep some of the other things but would send most of the other things back to my brother Mark. We probably would never see those four men again, but if we do, so be it. I was alone on the stage because I had gone on ahead while Katherina visited with an aunt whom she hadn't seen for some time.

That evening, I met Katherina in the small town I was headed for and where her aunt lives. I went to see the sheriff, as he was up at the county seat on official business when we arrived in town, and told him all about the other four men and gave them only a partial description as they were masked. Under the circumstances, I could not do anything about the attempt since my guns were in my bag on the top of the coach, and they had the drop on us. The other passengers told the sheriff the same thing I had, and he commended me for not trying anything while there was a possibility that someone could get hurt.

February 16, 1873

This morning, while we were still in that town, I was walking down the sidewalk. I saw a man riding toward me. His manner on the horse looked familiar, so I stopped and watched him ride by. At first, he didn't see me, but when he did, he went for his gun, upon which I drew mine. He was faster, but I was truer. It turned out that he was one of the four holdup men. One of the deputies was nearby and saw it go down and said that it clearly was self-defense. I didn't kill him, only wounded him, and he went to jail for attempted holdup of the stage and attempted murder, mine.

September 20, 1873

I was on the trail of one man when he became aware of my being after him. He had heard that there was someone looking for him but didn't know who or why, so he took cover to ambush me. His first shot knocked me off my horse, and the second one killed my horse. If it had not been for a small band of Sioux Indians who knew me and what I stood for, I would have died out there. They had also given me a name which roughly translates to *she who wears a badge*.

They had heard the shots and came to investigate and found me. They cared for my wound, which was a shoulder wound. Once I got into their camp, they all insisted that I take many of their horses, but since I only needed one horse, I chose a good one.

They took my belongings off my dead horse and brought them into camp while others went after the man who shot me. They knew that I would take him to the law for trial. When the Indians first brought him into the camp, he thought they were going to torture and kill him, but when he saw me, he realized that they were only helping me.

About a year ago, when I was on the trail of another man, I came across the tribe, half-starved, and killed several deer for them and talked to the government into letting them have two dozen rifles and all the ammunition that they needed to be able to hunt down their own meat. The man I was after at the time turned out to be the Indian agent, and he was responsible for them being half-starved. He had told the government that they were always on the warpath, and white men and women were always disappearing and turning up later dead. This was a lie; the people who were supposed to disappear never did exist in the first place.

The outlaw wanted to be able to have the land by running off the Indians by way of the government. My coming along put a stop to his efforts. He had found gold on the land (or so he thought) and wanted it all to himself, but white men could not dig in Indian territory. The Indians told me that they were aware of the yellow stuff, but it is what white men call fool's gold, as they were told by a trapper that went through the area some thirty summers ago. They even told the agent that it was fool's gold, but he would not believe it.

They had chosen not to make war on the whites because that trapper and others had helped them over the years, but they didn't stand by and let white men make war on them if they could help it.

And when I came along, they knew they had another friend in the white man's world, for I also helped them. That was when they gave me my Indian name. On this meeting, I found out that on several occasions, they even helped the army. That was after I had made it known that the agent was a liar.

January 15, 1874

About a week ago, while passing through the country around the Black Hills of South Dakota, I chanced to see a small group of Sioux Indians, an offshoot of the band that I helped two years earlier, and they helped me last year. One of them saw me and gave me the sign of recognition, and I returned it. As I watched them, I saw that they were having trouble turning a small heard of buffalo toward a cliff, but the leader just would not turn, and they could not get close enough to kill her. Upon seeing that, I dismounted and took my rifle and lay down to steady the shot. I took careful aim and killed the leader. With that, the herd turned into the direction the Indians wanted them to go and the herd plunged to their deaths and the tribe had winter food and cloths and teepees. The Indians knew the people in the nearby town had been sick, so they gave them some of the meat to help pay back a debt they owed, once again proving that not all Indians made war against whites.

That night, the Indians gave a feast, and I was the honored guest, along with some the men and women from town. Since I was with the people from town, I asked them to look over the lists of names that I had with me to see if there was any one in the town with those names, or maybe something similar, but there wasn't any. The Indians gave me a buffalo robe made out of the leader's hide since it was my bullet that brought her down and sent the herd on to the cliff and their death. I would not have interfered if they could have downed her, and they knew it. When the people left to go back to town, I gave the robe to one of the men and told him to submerge it in water for the next two days, then hang it out to dry. I told them I was going to stay in the village for two or three days then go to town for a look around, just in case there was someone there who would recognize me.

The second morning after the buffalo hunt, the new Indian agent came by to talk to the chief about the meat that was given to the town. When he heard that I was there, he wanted to see me and to thank me for all that I had done for the people. Because the Indians never gave him my white name, only my Indian name, he didn't know what it meant, and he was unafraid to come near me. The Indians didn't care too much for him, but he was an honest man, so unless one of the people or their blood brother or sister was being threatened by him, he was left alone.

When the man saw me, he went for his gun. When it cleared leather, one of the Indians threw his spear, killing him. In the meantime, another Indian who was standing near me stepped between me and him and took the bullet for me, but it did not kill him; he was my blood brother. A check of his personal belongings and papers proved that he was one of the two hundred men who I was after. After he was buried, the judge gave me all of our things that he still had, plus he gave me all of the man's things.

There were five men from the town there at the time, and they all testified that the Indians were defending me when they killed the agent. Two braves took our things back to our land, leaving all of the horses except the two they rode in on. One of the two had gone to our land before, so he knew where to take them. I wanted him to take the things because he had been there before and to show someone else where to go. Both he and the young man that went with him knows English.

I decided to keep the buffalo robe because I knew I would be needing it in a few more months. When summer comes, I would leave it in Silverton until the next time I would need it so that I could keep warm in the winter. The reason I had had one of the townsfolk submerge it for a few days is because I knew there were fleas on it, and I didn't want to get any sickness that fleas carry. Then we let the robe dry out for several days, while I looked around the town.

September 5, 1875

I was on the trail of one man, but his trail led to so many places that I was beginning to think that I would never catch up to him. I really had him spooked until he finally got tired of me dogging him. He knew it was me because he had caught sight of me on several occasions, so he took cover and shot me from ambush. Only he didn't get me; he got my horse, pinning my leg under her. In his attempt to leave the scene after the shooting, he fell and broke his leg, then a rattler got him on the other leg. Two hours later, a rancher on his way into town for supplies found us. He took me to the doctor to treat my leg and the man's body over to the undertakers. Then he took my things from off my horse and the man's horse and other things over to the livery.

Two weeks earlier, Kate had gotten sick and was laid up for a while, and I had gone on ahead upon her insistence because we had heard about this man, so she said that this man must pay for what he did. This injury in the leg would lay me up for a week, and it made this the second time my horse was killed, and I was injured. I was laid up for one week the other time too. Kate caught up with me while I was recovering from my injured leg.

June 30, 1876

We are in Leavenworth, Kansas. Yesterday afternoon, some men brought the news in that George Armstrong Custer, and his men of the Seventh Cavalry was massacred at the fork of the Little Bighorn River in the Dakota Territory. In this morning's *Leavenworth Star*, the local paper, there were more details about his death and the Indians who fought him. It said that there was a total of 225 officers and men who died that day, which was June 25. The article listed the names of the men of the seventh, starting with Colonel Custer, right down to the lowliest private and even the scouts.

Later that day, when I was on my way to lunch with Kate and the marshal, we were almost in front of the bank when we heard two shots come from the bank. Suddenly the door burst open, and four men came backing out. The moment they saw us, they turned to shoot us, but they were shot instead. All three of us had our guns drawn and ready when they came out, and all three of us opened fire on them.

November 1, 1876

I had followed one man to Goldfield, Nevada where he tried the same thing that the man tried in Fayetteville, North Carolina. He had gone to the sheriff not knowing that it was me following him. His trial had to be changed to another town because some years earlier, while I was traveling through here looking for some of the men, I helped clear the town of several outlaws who had taken over the town. The citizens tried several times to clear the town but just could not pull everyone together at the same time until I came along. Three of those outlaws turned out to be the same ones that brought me into the area. After they were arrested, they were tried and convicted and sentenced to hang. They were hung the next morning after the trial. The judge gave me all the stuff those three men had that was ours, which was very little. They could not add any more names to my list, even though they said that there was more, but they did take away two more names other than their own names.

One man went to San Francisco, California sometime in the spring of 1877 to see the sights, but I was never able to catch up to him. He had signed on to a ship to see the Orient. When he was on his way back to the States, he got drunk and started talking about his past, and one of the things he said was that he had taken part of the murder. After he sobered up, the captain of the ship questioned him, and he confessed to his part. Being out at sea, the captain was law, so he had the man's things put under lock and key until they got back to the States, whereupon he was turned over to the local law and his things were turned over to the San Francisco attorney general for distribution to all parties concerned.

Everything that he had that was ours was given back to me; the other things were given to his family. The things that he had picked up on the Orient were divided equally between his family and me. He had left a will leaving all of the things as the judge had given us. His family tried to fight the will because they wanted everything he had gotten from the Orient. There was also a map showing where some of our things were hidden. He had heard about my hunt and was prepared for it.

One man went to Mexico to hide. When I heard that he was down there, I went after him. When the Mexican police heard that I was looking for him and why, they let me have him. They did not want an American who kills women and children in their country, so I brought him back to the United States for trial. When I got him back across the border, I took him to the nearest town. There he was tried and convicted for murder and later was hung.

Three men went to England to inherit some money. They had gone over on the same ship, but only one returned. I took that one man into custody after he got off the ship and turned himself in to a minister for safe conduct to jail. He then told me one man stayed behind to take care of some other matters concerning his parents. The other man got on the ship to come back, but he fell overboard in a bad storm. I then went over to England to take the third man into custody, but he fell off the London Bridge upon seeing me. He thought he was seeing a ghost.

One man went to the Congo jungles of dark Africa in search of gold. He went over two years before the missionaries got into the area. Four years after the missionaries got there, I was able to follow his trail down there, and there I found his shrunken head on the trophy pole of one of the last unconverted headhunters. He was the last of the five men that I had seen, and I recognized him at the time.

The missionary told the people my story as I told it to him and he related it to how God's justice works and how if they don't get right with God before they die, they will be punished for eternity, just like I punished these men on earth. As a result, the last of the headhunters got saved, and the head was buried.

I followed the trails of several men as they led in or near Silverton. I found out that some of them had ranches close to our lands and close to town. Some even had businesses in town. They were making it very good around there, ignoring the threat of being hunted. They either didn't know, didn't care, or didn't think that I would come and get them. One man even told me he didn't think I could follow the trails. When I asked him why he thought that, he said that I am a woman and unless I was raised in the west, I could never do it. I showed him that he was wrong; I got him and all the others.

Two of the men who had ranches had sections of land that touched each other's sections and some of our own land, but they never knew that theirs touched ours, nor did I know it. I found that out after they died. Even so, their wills turned their lands over to us as I caught up to them, otherwise it would all go to their next of kin. With that, our land increased by several thousand acres. It stretched all the way from our campsite to Silverton, a four days' journey away. As a result, we decided to allow the near kin of the men to stay on as caretakers, since they had nothing to do with the attack.

We have also gained several pieces of property in other states, from ocean to ocean and from Canada to Mexico, including a few acres in each country of Canada and Mexico. One man's will even left us some property in England. Mark and I decided to sell the land in Canada, Mexico, and England so that we don't have to worry about fees in those countries or how they are being cared for. We also sold the land in most of the other states and some of the land around Silverton so that we won't have to worry about who is taking care of it.

May 19, 1879

Today since I was in the area, I had gone to Silverton to see my daughter and the other members of my family living there. We had gone into town to buy some things, and while there, some drunken cowboy came out of one of the saloons. When he saw me, he started shooting in my direction. He had gotten off five rounds before he was gunned down. I was unarmed at the time so I was not able to even defend my own family; the marshal was nearby, and he brought the man down. At first, I thought that everyone was all right, but one of those five got little Aaron in the lower back while he was trying to get out of the range of those bullets. The doctor who treated me that day also treated Aaron. He told me that he would be partially paralyzed in his left leg for the rest of his life. He would be able to walk but with a limp, and he would have to stay in bed for a while. It turned out that the drunk was one of the two hundred men who I was looking for and a brother to one of the men I had already caught.

July 22, 1879

Last week, one man followed me to Silverton in hopes of taking revenge for his brother's death. He figured that if I had not sent his brother to prison mistaking him for some other man, his brother would not have died of consumption and might still be alive today. I found out what he wanted to do, so I headed for the campsite, making sure the townspeople knew I wanted him to follow me but to make sure to keep him there until at least two days have passed before telling him where I went.

After I got to the campsite, I remained there until he arrived. After he got there, he stopped in front of the plaque because that is where I was standing, which was near the gate. I asked him what he saw, and he told me that he was looking at the cemetery and plaque. I told him that his brother's name was given to me by one of the men that I had seen before the attack. I also told him that his brother had thought that he had seen a ghost and fainted. I would not have arrested him if that had not happened.

The townspeople are the ones who had sent him to jail, not me. The only thing in his favor was that he neither killed any of these people nor did he take any of the possessions. I also told him that his brother was already sick when he was captured. After that, he told me his story, then he told me he was sorry, and we went our separate ways. I went back to town to let my family know that I was all right, and he went to the east. Would I hear about him again, maybe?

August 17, 1880

A few days ago, Kate and I had left Adobe Walls, Texas and traveled west. When we got into the area of Taos, New Mexico, we reached the crest of a small hill and overlooked one of the most beautiful sights there was to see. And I know because I have seen a lot of things in the last few years, and this is one sight that I will never tire of. I was looking at a wild horse roundup. While we were on the hill, the foreman saw us watching the action and came to see what we wanted. I showed him the badge and told him that we were just passing through and stopped to watch for a while. He told us any outsider who helps with the roundup is paid fifty dollars and the choice of any two horses after their own men have made their choices for their remounts, and we are welcome to join if we want to. We looked at each other and without saying a word, galloped down to help. We did it because the horses we were riding were beginning to get worn down, and we wanted to increase our own herd back home. We could also use the money to replenish our pocket change. We kept the stragglers together and within the herd.

After the horses were all corralled, the men separated all the young stallions from the mares. Then they separated the mares with colts from those without colts. With all that was done, they checked to see if anyone wanted the colts and mares. After the boss paid us, I selected a nice big young stallion and a really nice-looking mare that I had seen earlier. Kate selected two fine-looking mares, one of which had a colt. I decided to keep the mare I picked and Kate would keep one of her mares, and we would send our own horses with the mare that had the colt and the stallion back to our land in Colorado.

After all of that, they let the big king stallion and the rest of the mares with colts and two or three of the other mares, go back to the hills. They said that they did that every couple of years to keep down the wild horse herd and to replenish their own working stock. What they didn't keep, they would sell to the army and other ranchers. What they did keep was for working and breeding stock. We told them we would like to stay on for a few days while we broke our horses, and the boss said we could.

The foreman had told his boss later that the two of us were responsible for more than ten good horses not getting away, young mares and stallions, one of which I had gotten because I liked the way she stood. The boss paid us each an additional twenty dollars and asked us to join him and his family for supper, of which we accepted. He even said he would put us up in his house so that we would be away from his men because he didn't want to tempt them.

After supper, the three of us went into another room while his wife and daughters cleared the dishes. I told him my story and showed him the badge and papers that had the names on. After reading the names, he took his pencil and marked off a name about halfway down on the third page. He said that it was his kid brother, and when his brother returned in November of 1869, his brother had a number of things with him, but he was not right in the head, and he kept having nightmares. When the boy was pressed about everything going on, he broke down and told them what he had done.

The next morning, he showed us his brother's grave. The stone gave his brother's name, when he was born, and when he died. That evening, our host gave me back our stuff that the boy had brought with him. After a week working with the horses, we were able to continue on to Taos, New Mexico, so that I could see if my source was right about there being a man whom I had on my list. Of course, there was no one there because it was the young man back at the ranch. But I did get conformation that the kid was tried and convicted of murder even though I was not there to testify against him. And so we moved on to hunt for those men, never knowing where a trail would lead us.

February 3, 1881

Yesterday, we followed the trail of one man into Evergreen, Kansas. We went to the marshal as we always did, but he arrested me and accused us of stealing the badge and papers because he was of the opinion that women cannot be badge totters. I told the marshal the whole story of what happened to me and how I came to have the authority to carry the badge, but he did not believe me. Word had gotten around town that he had arrested us and why, and the next morning, one of the town's leading ranchers came in, bringing in one of his men. The man told the marshal that he had been involved with the attack. With that the marshal opened the cell door and let us out, then he put the other man in the cell. The marshal returned our stuff to us, and he apologized, and that we could go anytime we wanted.

Even though it was a mistake, we were gone just as soon as we could get our horses saddled up, just in case someone hadn't heard that we had been set free. One of the deputies was sent along so that the man at the livery would know that we hadn't escaped. That man's name was crossed off the list, and his share of our things was sent to our place in Silverton.

September 2, 1882

Back in 1865, just before my fifteenth birthday, I had come down with smallpox. That had given me a lifetime of immunity, and I was glad because this morning, we arrived in a small town in Wyoming and found out that they were having an epidemic of small pox there. Kate had never been exposed to it until the day we rode in. She became quite ill, but under my care, she recovered. I also helped out with other people in town that was sick. To help a person recover, they have to be kept covered and their faces cool.

I had been telling them to post people at all the roads in to keep people out until the epidemic was passed, but no one wanted to do it until an Indian from a nearby village came into town, and he too was exposed to the sickness. That is when they finally posted guards, but not until he had gone back to his village. No one wanted to go to care for his people, so I had to until they were out of danger. The Indians were Arapaho, and they welcomed me to their village.

Toward the end of the Indian epidemic, when there was only a few still sick but out of danger, one of the braves saw the necklace that I got from the Sioux, and they took me for the enemy. I had some difficulty getting them to believe that I was there to help, not spy them out for the Sioux. They were just about to kill me when I gave them my Sioux name which translated to *she who carries a badge*. Three braves who had been captives of the Sioux for a while stepped in front of me and repeated the name in the Arapaho tongue, and they all put down their weapons. After that, they honored me by making me one of their tribe. They gave me a necklace to wear along with the other necklace, and their name for she who carries a badge. They also gave me four of their best horses picked from the whole herd.

Many of the braves had heard about me when they would pay visits to the white man's towns, but they always thought that the stories were about a legend, like they have in their tribes. Even though their legends are based on fact, they thought those stories were made up. After the tribe had honored me, I told them which ones of the stories about me was true and which one was not true. They were enjoying hearing them, and I could have gone on for several more days, but I had to get back to town so that I could continue my quest.

When I returned to town, Kate told me about an old man who lives on the outskirts of town, and that while he was still sick, he kept babbling about the attack on my family. Kate, the sheriff, and the doctor all took me to where the old man lives. When he saw me, he had a heart attack and died. The doctor said that he had a weak heart as a result of the fever but should have been able to live a few more years if he took care of himself.

Both the doctor and sheriff testified that I never touched the man. In going through his things, the sheriff found a confession of what he did to us, why he did it, and where he hid his share of our things. After the judge saw and heard everything, he said that I was free to take all of our things back, but if there was another living relative, they would get his things. If there was no one else, his things would be sent to our ranch. Upon leaving that town, I continued my search for the killers. When will it ever end?

May 17, 1883

Kate and I arrived in Deadwood, South Dakota this afternoon. We put our horses up at the livery stable and headed up the street toward the marshal's office to let him know we were in town and will be for a few days because we had heard that there were a couple of men there that might be on my lists. After seeing the marshal, we headed over to the hotel to get a couple of rooms. As we were entering the hotel, some man gave the sign of recognition, but he came over and gave me a hug and said he was glad to see me alive and well and wanted to know how many others survived that day. I told him that I was the only adult survivor, and the two infants also survived.

I asked him when it was that he saw me, and he explained that he was one of the two hundred, but when he heard what they were going to do, he tried to talk the men out of it. They did not want to hear any more from him, so they hit him over the head and knocked him out. When he came to, the shooting was over, and he rode in to try to stop them from taking the lives of the two infants and kept them from shooting the wounded again. When the men left, he stayed until he saw the buffalo hunters coming, but it was before the hunters got there.

After that, he took off for parts unknown; until I came along, he thought he was clear of the men. I told him that one of the men that I caught gave me his name, and he thought it was for spite. When I heard that, I told him that as far as I was concerned, he was not part of the event, only a person who came along after the fact. He told me his name and crossed it off my list with a notation that he was never part of the two hundred. After we checked in to the hotel, I went back to the marshal and told what had happened, and he agreed that that man was not part of the attack.

February 29, 1884 (Leap year)

Kate and I tracked two men into Nashborough, Tennessee. Kate had told me that she had a brother and a cousin with names just like two of the names that I had on my list, but we were hoping that they were not the same two. But upon seeing me, they gave the only reaction anyone could give had they been involved. Kate asked them how deeply they were involved in the shooting. They told us that they had done some of the shooting and that they have got some of the things that they took. They told us that they did it because their leader had said that we were a bunch of thieves and that they would be doing the country a favor by getting rid of us. The only thing in their favor was that they did not shoot any of the women and children; they drew the line at that.

Kate lost her father, a brother, a sister, and a few cousins in the attack by the Indians. There were two sisters and five brothers to survive that attack.

April 15, 1884

It was six weeks ago that Kate and I sent her brother and cousin to jail for being a party to killing my family. Yesterday morning,

Kate told her mother what we did and why, and her mother forgave her for what we did to them; it had to be done. We stayed all of yesterday, and she invited us to stay a few days, so we did. This morning, we went to the sheriff to see if any of the men we were after was here and to let him know that we were in town mainly to visit with Kate's mother.

Later, after wandering the streets for a few hours, I went to a restaurant to have a bite to eat. One man came in, looked at me, and turned around and went right back out. A few minutes later, he came back with the sheriff and pointed right at me. But instead of coming over and arresting me, he arrested that man. After a few minutes, the sheriff came back and told me that, that man had gone to him and said that there was a wanted killer in town. When he pointed me out, the sheriff knew that he was one of the men I was after, so he arrested the man to be held for trial when the judge would get in town in a few days. That gave me another reason to stay on in town.

When the judge got in and the trial was held, the man was found guilty of murder and sentenced to hang. The man had no family, no personal belongings to speak of, and none of our things anymore. When asked why he tried to say that I was a wanted killer, he said that I had been out hunting down many of his friends and wanted it to stop.

June 21, 1884

We followed the trail of one man to the shores of the Mississippi. At first, he wouldn't believe that I had come after him; a woman just would not do such things. The judge sent him to jail and to hang. Later we heard that there was another man down in New Orleans, so we booked passage on a riverboat with our horses and went down the river. Upon arriving there, we had some difficulty finding him. We found out that he was Cajun, and his people did not want to give him up without proof that he did what I said he did. I told them that if he had a look at me, it would be proof enough. With one look at me, he tried to shoot me, but his people defended me, and he was sent to jail. Both his things and that of the man's that we captured up river were sold, and the money went to their kin. Our things were sent back to Silverton after we got them back.

November 18, 1884

It has been two months since we left New Orleans and headed west. This morning, we were on a train going back to San Antonio, Texas, following the trail of one man as it leads from New Orleans. At the last stop before the sun came, two men got on. Since everyone was asleep, they paid no attention to anyone and settled in for their ride. Kate and I were in a sleeper car, so they didn't even know we were on the train. Later, I got up, fixed myself up, and went to the dining car for my breakfast, leaving Kate sleeping. A few minutes later, the men came in and sat down at the other end of the car, and one of them was facing me. I was holding up my menu, ordering my breakfast, so they didn't see me at first.

After placing the menu on the end of the table, I saw them but paid no attention to them. One of the two men saw me and studied me for some, trying to place where he had seen me before, while the other man had been to Silverton and knew my story. The first man asked the second if he knew who I was. The man turned around and looked at me and told the first one who I was. With that, he jumped to his feet, drew his gun, and shot twice at me, yelling, "Let me finish the job we started years ago."

When he cleared his holster, I dove under the table because I was unarmed. Another man that was wearing his gun drew and fired, killing the man with his only shot. Luckily, that man was a Texas Ranger stationed in San Antonio.

I explained to him that there were originally two hundred men who might want me dead. But many of them are either dead themselves or in prison, although there are still quite a few still on the loose somewhere. There are also a few of their kinfolk who might feel the same way. The dead man's name was marked off my list by his partner.

His shots wounded another man but not seriously. Up until the shooting ended, Kate was still in the sleeper car. The shots woke her up. When she came out, I had to explain to her what all the shooting was all about. At that, she sat down and ordered her meal too. In San Antonio, I found out that the man that we were chasing had gone up to Abilene, Texas. So that's where we would go next.

When we headed north, we came across the cattle drive of a friend of ours that had said that we could join one of his drives anytime we were in the area and going the same direction. We decided that since his offer was always open, we would join up with him and help him drive his herd to Abilene. We would be going along the old Chisholm Trail. It took us two weeks for us to get to Abilene. When we got there, we found the man we were after and killed him. We had no choice; in spite of the fact that when I saw that he had recognized me and I already had drawn my gun and the sheriff was right there with us, he still went for his gun trying to kill me. He had suspected that somebody was after him. He didn't know until that time that I was the one chasing him.

Leaving there, we followed the trails of what we thought were some of the men we were after, but each time we went to a town, we found out that we were wrong—right name, wrong men. I knew that they had nothing to do with the attack because they did not give the sign that they recognized me. But we did eventually find those men who we were after. In a way, we were glad of the fact that we were wrong because we didn't like hunting down the men.

We kept going though and ended up in Sacramento, California before any of our leads came true. We found a man there enjoying the riches his father had worked for and had combined it with our things and had become even richer. He had told his father that he had married a Southern girl, but she died on her way out here. It was September of 1885 when we got into Sacramento. His father had died a few years ago, not knowing the truth.

After that, the judge sent him to jail, and I got our things back. While here, I heard a rumor that one man was up in Alaska, but it is too close to winter, so we have decided to stay in the area for the winter and go up next spring. Sacramento is the town where John A. Sutter had set up a trading post and colony and had become rich, but when James W. Marshall found gold at the mill he was building on Sutter's land, he lost everything to the gold hunters. This all happened in 1848, which was too bad because he had quite a spread.

March 20, 1886

This was the trail of the man who went up to Alaska. He had heard of gold being up here, not finding any in California. He also had heard that I was chasing the men who attacked my family and thought that he would be safe up here. When we got here, I discovered that he had filed on one of the richest deposits of gold in that area, but two months after he had filed on his claim, when he was going from his claim to town like he did every weekend, the cold got him. That spring, just one month before I got here, he was found just fifty feet from one of the town's buildings, frozen solid, not a mark on him, showing that the cold did get him. He had left a will turning two-thirds of his gold mine over to me. The rest of his mine went to his nieces and nephews. All of our personal things were gone; he used them to stake his claim.

I had heard from several different people that he had cheated a man out of his half of the gold, so after checking into the story to see if it was true and to make sure that he was not one of the men that attacked my family, I gave him half of my share so that the gold could be mined and sold. My share of the money would go into the bank in Silverton for my family and myself. We would spend one month up here to look around and make all the arrangements for the mine.

July 1, 1886

It has been two months since we left Alaska. This week, we allowed another young lady to join us. Her name is Dawn, and she is a first cousin to a set of twins who was with us on the wagon train. She is nineteen now and will help us hunt down the rest of the men. She will also do some of the things that we are beginning to have trouble doing because of our age. After all, it has been sixteen years since we started the hunt. Also we would not have allowed her to join if she had not been related to someone on the wagon train. Sometime back, one of Kate's family members had asked to join us later on, and we had said yes, but so far the occasion has not occurred.

Whenever Sunday came and we were on the trail, we would remain there all day until Monday, singing and meditating on the Lord's words from the Bible. If I came close to a town, I would stay there and go to church on Sunday if there was a church of my faith, otherwise I would remain in the hotel until Monday. Kate and Dawn's beliefs were not as strong as mine, but we respected each other's beliefs.

Before we started on the hunt, I had explained myself to Kate so that we could get along better. At first, she couldn't get used to my habits, but as time went on, she has gotten used to them. She would go to church with me but never remained in the hotel with me. She would go to the sheriff or marshal and let them know that we were in town, and she would look the town over. That evening when she got back, she remained quiet about what she found out in the town until the next day. I wanted to continue the same practice that we had done while we traveled before the attack.

When Dawn joined us, she already understood me even though she didn't believe as strong as me. She too would go with me to church and she would go with Kate to look the town over and like Kate, she would remain quiet until Monday. At that time, I would go introduce myself to the sheriff or the marshal, whichever the case may be. Then I would go look the town over to see what the people did when they saw me.

On one occasion, just a little over twenty-five years after the attack and my hunt started, we walked into a church in Fort Detroit, Michigan and sat down in the back, as I always do. The preacher had seen me enter and welcomed us as visitors to the services, and everyone turned around to see the visitors. As soon as the services were over, two men got up and left as fast as they could. After the hand shaking was over, I went back to my hotel room, leaving only long enough to eat, and Kate and Dawn went about their usual thing. They had gone to the sheriff to talk about the men. But again, since it was my policy not to talk about the hunt to anyone, they did not tell me about the two men and waited until Monday.

On Monday morning, they told me that the two men had gone over to the sheriff's office and turned themselves in, and I went to the sheriff to talk to him about the men. The sheriff told me that we will have to stay on for a few days for the trial. Of course we were going to stay on anyway to look for other men involved in the attack. There was one more man there, and he got what the other two men got, death.

December 22, 1888

This morning, while in Portland, Oregon, I received two letters by way of Mark. One came from New York and the other came from Boston from the high society ladies' clubs of those two cities. They said that they were reviewing the recommendations for membership from the past and found that I had been recommended for membership, but I refused for reasons of my own. Upon further investigation, it was discovered that the reason I turned them down was that I wore a badge. They know that I still wear a badge, but they are willing to overlook that fact and make me an honorary lifetime member of their clubs. No dues need ever be paid, and attendance at meetings are not mandatory.

I am getting tired of hunting the men, but I must go on. I have the authority to do so, and I am the only one who can throw any fear into them. Anyone else and they would deny any involvement in the attack. I will go on until I find the last of them. It has taken me twenty-one years to find one hundred and twenty-five of the men. Almost all of the outlaws were captured or killed by other people who knew that they were wanted by the law or me or both. In these twenty-one years, I have gone across the United States more times than I can count on both hands. Up to Alaska and Canada twice, down to Mexico once. Twice across the Atlantic, once to Europe, and once to Africa. It is unknown at this time just how long we have yet to find the other twenty-five men that are still out there, and when we will find them. This is worse than when we were looking for our new land. On top of that, I was much happier then. I had all of my family with me; I am almost the last one left.

My daughter Amy Sue and my nephew Aaron IV had been left in Silverton with my brother and his family so that he can take care of them while I was gone. He has a son and a daughter of his own, and he and his family had come to Silverton while I was still recovering. After my husband's death, he agreed to take care of the two babies even before I told him about my desire to hunt those men down, since I was the only one who could identify any of them, and any fear or surprise could be thrown into the others. He was there to support me when my husband was buried in the town cemetery and later when all of the bodies were taken out to the campsite to be placed alongside the others.

When I would go visit Amy and the others, I would always teach Amy and Aaron that even though everyone else died and I almost died myself, I no longer hate any of the men, but I did at first. That hatred died even before I started the hunt. I am using the law to make them pay for what they did to us. Her uncle Mark has the same loss as I do, and he defends what I am doing. Since the years have taken its toll on them and us, we just feel sorry for them. They must pay, that is why the hunt must go on.

June 15, 1889

Last evening, after checking into our hotel rooms, Kate got word by telegram that her mother had passed. Anytime we would arrive in a town, we would let my brother know where we are so that he can let us know if there is any news for any of us; that is how Kate got word. We all decided to stay on here for one day, not looking for the men, so Kate could mourn for her mother. Last night, Kate did a lot of remembering of all the good things and the bad where her mother was concerned. All the good times they had together. She even had a dream that her mother had been killed in the Indian attack, but she knew better. Later, she remembered even more things including the two times we visited with her after we started my search. This evening while we were having our dinner, Ned Buntline approached me and offered a deal to put me in one of his books, but I declined his offer and told him I wasn't doing this for fame—I just wanted justice.

April 21, 1890

It is twenty-six years after the attack. We followed the trail of one man to Philadelphia, Pennsylvania. We discovered that he was very popular there. He even served as chief of police and mayor while there. Because of all the good things that he did, no one close to him believed that he was one of the men that we were after. He even told them that he was one of the men, but they would not let him go. He knew that they cared deeply about him, so in front of his best friends and the subchief, and so that I would not be accused of killing him to get revenge, he took his own life with a gun that he had hidden in his desk drawer.

He left behind a full confession and a will leaving to me all of the things that he had taken from my family. He left all of the things that he had gained over the years to local charities, with a few thousand dollars to me for user fees since our things were what made him rich in the first place. Finally he left his second home and the furnishings inside to his family because they were his before he attacked my family. He had talked to me about his will so that I would not have to change it later, as it was my idea to leave his original home to his children, even if they did not like his new home going to charities.

In spite of the confession, a lot of the townspeople still would not believe it, nor could they believe that he could take part in such an evil thing after all the good things that he did. He stated to the sheriff that after he had taken part in the killing, he realized that he did wrong and that he did everything possible to make up for it except go to jail, even though he knew that he should. Ironically, the very moment of his death, I was talking to the chief of police, telling him that I am leaving there and that someday he will pay

for his part of the attack. I will leave him to the Lord and go on to
the next man.

Even though he was with the subchief and I was with the chief,
some of the townspeople tried to say I murdered him and brought
charges against me, but they didn't stick because of the witnesses.

June 28, 1890

Two days ago, while I was trailing one of the men, which was among
the last three men, a snake scared my horse and made him bolt. Since
he was an old horse, I was not expecting it, and he threw me. My
shoulder hit a rock, injuring me badly. A band of gypsies that was
camped nearby heard the noise and came running. They found me
and took me to their camp to take care of me for the night.

The next morning, I told them who I was and that I was after a
man who had taken part in the death of my family. They told me
that they had seen the man I was chasing. Two days earlier, while
in that same spot, a man came through who was constantly looking
back as if he was trying to see if there was someone right behind
him. They had given him shelter for the night and that was when
he gave them his name. They then gave me that name, and I knew
just how close I was to catching up with him. That was the man
that I was seeking.

Kate was sick again with the flu, the third time, so she had sent
me on ahead to see if I could catch this man. A week earlier, we
had sent Dawn on ahead to see if she could find a trace of another
man. The two of them were to meet me back in Silverton in a week.
I was four days' journey away from there right now, and I would
be glad to get back there to see the town again. It had been a long
time since I last saw Amy and the others. The gypsies would let me
go with their blessings of encouragement; they also gave me a few
gemstones to help me if I need help. Many people believe that a

gypsy's blessing is good luck, and I guess it is so because the men that Dawn and I were chasing ended up in Silverton.

September 10, 1890

This morning, while traveling through Michigan, just south of where the lakes Huron and Michigan join, I was alone again as Kate and Dawn had gone on ahead to look for clues on the whereabouts of the last man. As I crested a hill, I saw, just a few hundred yards ahead and to my right, three men had tied an Indian brave to a tree and was beating him up. When I rode up, I asked them what they were doing, and they said that it was none of my business, that they can handle things here. I told them that if it was a matter of the law that it was my business, and I would handle it.

One of them had started to come over to me with the look that a man would have toward a woman. With that, I moved my hand in a way that would pull my coat aside and reveal both my badge and gun. With that he stopped for a moment and looked closer at me, then he went for his gun, but he wasn't fast enough. The bullet went through his gun arm. The other two men had seen what happened but would not go for their guns. A fourth man had heard the shot and came running out of the bushes with his pants halfway down to his knees and a gun in his hand. When he saw me, he dropped his gun and continued to pull up his pants. I made two of them untie the Indian and lay him down, and then I tied up the four men. When I bent down to care for the Indian, he said that he was with his wife, and I knew that I needed to look in the bushes where the other man came out of.

Just a few feet beyond the bushes, I found a young woman, lying unconscious and naked. With that, I went back and got my blanket and covered her. While caring for her, a few warriors from their tribe rode up and saw me with the woman, but they only saw me from the back. They thought that I was the one that assaulted her, so one brave grabbed my gun at the same time that he and another brave grabbed my arms and pulled me up and away from her. They dragged me over to another brave who appeared to be the leader. The brave started to hit me for attacking the woman, but something made him stop and take a closer look at me. When he saw that I was a woman, he told the two that held me to release me and to give me back my gun. At first, they didn't want to, but when they too realized that I was a woman, I was released and given back my gun. At that, I went back to caring for the woman.

One of the other braves had found the injured brave and the four men tied up, and they all were about to kill the four when I told them that they would be punished the white man's way. I told them that I will take them to town, and I would like to have some of his braves to help me take these men to Justice. That is also the name of the town nearby so that they would get their justice for rape, assault, attempted murder, and for that one man, attempted murder of a peace officer.

While I took care of the woman, I checked on the young brave to see if he was okay. I told the braves that he will be all right in a few hours, but the woman needed help that I couldn't give her. We needed to rig up a travois for me to take her with us to town, and they agreed too. The young brave would come along with us to be near his wife. All the other braves will come to.

When we got into town, the people all came out to see what was going on. When they heard what the men had done, they took them straight to jail and the woman to the doctor. The doctor took her up to his office where he gave her special medicines for the different injuries. The doctor confirmed rape, as I knew, and told her husband that the men will be punished, and that his wife needs his support; just don't push his affections on her before she is ready.

At the trial, all four men were found guilty as charged. The reason the one drew on me was because I killed his brother. He did not know that his brother had taken part in the attack on my family, or he would not have drawn on me. All four men were sent to jail.

When the Indians left town, they were satisfied that justice was done. They knew that the townsfolk would do right by them because they had, had dealings there before. These Indians are of the Ojibwa tribe. And before I left, the young woman was up and around. She gave me her name, and it sounded like Laughing Waters. It was a beautiful name, but I gave her the name Terry. Even the townsfolk started calling her that, and she accepted it because it was the name I gave her.

April 13, 1891

We caught the last man this morning. Dawn was with us five and a half years, and we caught the last seven men together. Dawn would be heading back home to South Carolina to take care of her aged mother. Her mother's younger sister had been taking care of her mother, but she could no longer care for her as she too was growing older. She told me that would like to come out and live with me after her mother and her aunt had passed on, and I told her that it would be a pleasure to have her company in my retirement. All these years of the hunt, having these two fine ladies around had brought me joy and gave me the courage to go on. Although there were times when I thought I might lose their companionship because they thought they had found Mr. Right, only to find out that the man was related to someone I had put in jail or killed. They wanted to get to me through Kate or Dawn.

Sometimes the men would tell me where some of the others were last seen or heard of and that would go in their favor. Some added several names, but others could not add any. Then after I had compiled the entire list and had found all the men on one sheet, I would send that sheet back to Mark so that it could be added to the other things that I collected and sent back there. The names on each sheet were numbered, and every time I sent the things back, they would have a corresponding number so that Mark would know where they had come from.

Of the two hundred men, forty became lawmen of some sort; eighty went into business, either for themselves or others, including stores, banks, and ranches; thirty became wanderers, scouts, and other things; and fifty became outlaws. Some had gone through their share like water through a funnel. Others had been able to hang on to the things, and they became rich off it.

Some of the men, when they heard that I was on the hunt for them, made out their wills and left everything to my brother and his family and the other two survivors of the attack. Some of them stipulated in their wills that if I killed them, I personally would not get any of their riches, only the others would get anything. We also would get back our things. The men that were not killed went straight to jail for their part. Most of them were later hung, a few of them died of natural causes, and a few were beaten up in jail for taking part in the attack.

Anytime a man's will left all of his riches to us and I found out that he had a family and his will would leave them penniless, I would make arrangements with a local lawyer to have the family get back everything that he had before our things made him richer. I never let my hunt deprive anyone of a way to live except for the men I sought.

Every so often, those accounts would hit the papers even though I did not want them to, and it would bring me more fame than I cared for. It also brought me more respect, honor, and praise from people I have met, and hatred from those I sought.

Ten years ago when we were in Silverton, Mark told me that a railroad company wanted to buy a right-of-way through our land that would run north and south, but he put them off until I came to see them. After looking over their three choices, I decided on the central route, since it was the only route that would not be within sight of the campsite, but close enough so that those who wanted to see the sight could go and see it without having to travel more than ten hours to get there and back, and still be able to get a good look at it.

Mark said that it might be a good idea to sell all of the sections of land west of the tracks, and I agreed to it and told him to go ahead with the sale and allow twenty square miles of land, ten on either side of the tracks, to be sold for a town, with the closest point being a five-hour ride from our campsite. Five years ago I had heard that the town council had gotten together and voted on the name of the town. After only a few minutes of deliberation, they decided on the only logical name there could be. They named the town Sagebrush, part of it came from my name, and the other part because that is what is all around the town. I was very proud that they had chosen that name; after all it was me.

I also heard that they had requested and was granted that copies of all of the paintings and statues of me be made and the originals be sent to Sagebrush. Many of those things were put in different buildings around town. The life-size statues of me on horseback were placed at the major points around town; the rest was put in front of and inside of buildings. The smaller statues and paintings were placed in the government buildings and the banks and the post office.

This afternoon after Dawn left, I bought two one-way tickets to Sagebrush, Colorado. The ticket agent told me the town's complete history, not knowing I was the one the town was named after; I just let him ramble on. He said that if I was lucky, and nothing happens to her, I might catch a glimpse of Becky and her companions. He said all that unaware that he was talking to Becky, and I didn't tell him any different, nor did Kate.

THE RETIREMENT

April 14, 1891

I T TOOK US five hours to get here by train. Thirty years ago, it took four days to go that far by wagon train. When we got there, we saw quite a town. The main hotel, the largest saloon, the first bank, and a few other buildings were called Becky's; other locations around town are called Kate's, Katherina's, Amy's, Aaron's, and a few were even named Dawn's, but mostly Becky's because of me. Kate and I went to the hotel and registered to spend two nights there since it was a Saturday night.

The marshal got wind of our being in town and came to talk to us. He told us that we had his full cooperation to try and find any of the men we were looking for. I told him thanks, but the hunt was over; the last man was found a week ago and was waiting for the gallows. All were either dead or sitting in jail, some waiting for execution. I was no longer a marshal, even though I still had the badge and papers. I had sent in my resignation and a request to keep them, but that would depend on the present Washington, DC, judges. I still had the authority to hunt all the men down, but I was on my way home for good.

I told him that I would like some peace and quiet, and if it's possible, to station a guard at each end of the hallway and one in front of my door, and thus he did. The guards were to keep away troublemakers and sightseers away from my door. The one in front of my door would go to church with me on Sunday. Also he placed two guards outside in the alley. I would be guarded twenty-four hours a day until I leave. Before I leave, I would talk to each of the men and thank them personally for what they were doing and give them a photo of us. That way they can tell their kids and grandkids they met me and guarded me while I was in town. The reason for so many guards was that if someone did start to harass me, one man could escort him away, and there would still be two guards near my room.

April 18, 1891

This morning, before we left for the house that Mark, Amy, and the others had prepared for us, a photographer who had been in town for a few weeks hoping to get some pictures of me approached me and asked if he could get some pictures, and I said yes. I told him to have two copies made and to give one to the residents of Sagebrush and the other to the residents of Silverton, and he can tell them it will be titled "The Retirement" and that he got it direct from me. I also gave the story of my retirement to the local newspaper office here in Sagebrush, but I asked them to sit on the story for three days, which would give us time to get to our land and get settled in a little, which they agreed to. I had given the story to the newspaper in Silverton when we passed through and asked them to sit on it for a week; they agreed to it too.

With Mark driving a two-seater buckboard, we arrived at our new home late in the afternoon. Amy knew we were coming and had the best meal she could fix for us. When we rode in, the curtains in the front were drawn tight so it made the house a little dark, so we were surprised about the big meal. After the meal, she escorted us to our rooms, both on the main floor but in the back. She said that there was a third room back there for our other friend if she decided to join us. Her family would be using the second floor so that we could have the peace and quiet. It sure felt good not to have to worry about when we go to bed and what time to get up or to hunt down any more men. There would be no more getting up early in the morning unless we wanted to.

Later that evening after our meal, we were all sitting there talking when a messenger from Sagebrush brought me a cable from Washington, DC. The judges had voted unanimously that I should keep the badges, but I would be taken off the records as being a marshal with deputies. Tomorrow morning, the badges would go into the buildings that represent the last few years of the hunt.

October 4, 1891

At about noon this morning, one man came riding up and asked for me. When I came out, he told me I had one minute to tell him that I was not the one who shot his father, and if I was the one, then why did I do it. I told him that I might have. I was responsible for the deaths of a little more than two hundred men, some by accident, but most through the law. Those still alive would soon die, and the reason was about a quarter mile behind him next to two wagons. He said he was going to look around; if he was not satisfied, he would be back. He never came back, so I never knew if I had killed his father. He never gave me his name or even his father's.

October 15, 1891

A week has passed since that man rode in, and I had to go over to Silverton on business and found the man that had talked to me last week. He kept bragging about how he had gone out to kill me, but was outdrawn by me and lived to tell about it, but no one believed him. One of the other men saw me and asked him if he killed Becky since she didn't shoot him, and he said no because the method she used to outdraw him was with words. He had gone out there to kill her for killing his father, and would have too but could not because of what she said and did. Then he repeated everything that I said a week earlier. Then when he looked the place over, he realized that the stories he had heard were true, and he rode away without going back. The man who had seen me then turned and asked me if that is true, and I told them yes, it is true, and everyone laughed, including the man. They thought he was lying to make himself famous. They also thought that he had killed me. Later, he came to me and told me that he had seen me around town and decided to tell the story one more time so that I could confirm his story. He knew that they doubted him. He also knew that I was in the room at the time of his brag.

December 24, 1891

As you can guess by the date, it is Christmas Eve. In all of the years of the hunt, I had spent only three Christmases here with my family. This will be the first Christmas after the hunt that I will be with them, but Lord willing, not the last one. About 75 percent of the time, I never knew where I would be at Christmas. Many times it was on the trail, but there were times I could have Christmas in a town. When I was on the hunt, I would spend Christmas Day just like my Sundays—no travel or hunting until the day was over and the next day had come. Amy also gave me a grandson earlier in the month, and she named him after her daddy. She told me that if she ever has a girl, she will name her after me.

When Amy was eighteen years old, I heard that there was a big two-story house in the vicinity of where the campsite was on that fateful day. I was a little upset until I got back and found out that that Amy had asked a contractor to build the house there, but it was a quarter of a mile away. She and her family are living there to protect the area. Amy also had the contractors build on the back of her house a small three-bedroom apartment for me and my companions. They were for me and my friends when I would come and visit, and for when I retire from the hunt, when all the men are behind bars or dead.

She explained too that one family member in each generation will live in the house to protect the area. The choice will be made by each set of parents who live in the house when the children of that generation reach maturity. All other houses have to be built no closer than half a mile to be able to protect the area. Amy wants it that way, and it has my blessings.

June 30, 1892

This morning, as I was leaving by the back door of the house which is where my quarters are, I saw off in the distance some smoke and dust mixed together. I got on Amy's awaiting horse and rode out to see what was going on and found some of my neighbors, whose ranch borders mine, were harassing a band of gypsies. I asked my neighbors what they were doing, and they told me that they were trying to make them leave our land. I told them that they are right, this is our land, and we will decide who goes and stays, and anybody is welcome here as long as they abide by our rules. I also told them that the gypsies are welcome here anytime, since they saved my life once, and for our neighbors to get off our land.

After the neighbors left, I went over to talk to their leader and found out that this is the very tribe that helped me out a few years ago. I talked to them for a while then told them our rules, which is no campsite any closer than theirs, and no loud noises near the cemetery. They agreed and told they would behave. When I got back with Amy's horse, I explained to her what was going on and who was on our land. After she heard that, she said she was glad to hear that everything was settled. Later, she rode out to their camp and welcomed them herself.

July 1, 1892

Yesterday when the gypsies had arrived, they didn't tell me that there was anything wrong, but this morning, the chief of the gypsies told me that they needed my help. They had bought some land, and someone else is claiming the land also. So I had Mark look into the claim of both groups and found out that somebody had sold the same section to two different groups. Mark said that the land in question was part of our land, so we went out to talk to the other family. After almost an hour, the other family finally believed us when we told them that we owned the land, but that we would be willing to turn over to each of them sections of our land to farm, but not here, this is too close to the original campsite.

Each of the parties agreed to go two miles in opposite directions making this point the boundary between the two properties. The first group would go to the east, and the gypsies would go to the west. Each group would own one quarter mile per person over the age of fifteen. Both parties agreed since the number of people was equal. Also the strip in question is to remain in my possession as a boundary. So with that, Mark and I rode back to the ranch and relaxed to a great lunch.

When I got back home from the hunt, I began pointing out to Amy where each of the missing wagons were sitting at the time of the attack, and where the horses were tied. I also showed her where I was walking from and to and the position I had reached when I was shot. I could do so because that awful day is still fresh in my mind, as if it happened only yesterday, even though it has been years ago. Each time I showed her something, she marked it for future reference.

The cemetery is just north of where the horses were tethered. The horses were on the west side just outside of the circle of wagons. We always tied them on the west side so that we would know where the setting sun was at all times. We wanted to be able to go in that direction in the morning, and it became a habit. The big house was a quarter mile south of where the circle was, close enough for the family inside the house to see the place, but not so close as to mess up the area. Aaron has a big house about a quarter mile west of the campsite, and Mark has one north of there, and all houses were built by the same company.

Everything that the men left behind that day, except the wagons, was placed in a special building that was constructed two hundred and fifty yards east of the campsite. The wagons that were left behind were left in their original positions. The wagon and harness that the men used to carry us into town was put in a corner of the building. All of our things that I retrieved during my hunt were placed in other buildings that were constructed as needed. Each building was built a little further east of the previous building. They also ended up building several other buildings, some of which housed some of the things that was willed to us because I sent back so much stuff.

Many of the personal things that the men owned and were turned over to us, along with many of their guns, riding gear, and other things, along with the lists that I sent back, were placed in the other buildings that were built there. Things that other people gave us for helping them were placed in still other buildings. The lists were placed in the first building with a reference to which building their things were in and where. Each of the buildings was marked with signs telling what is on the inside. If there was any livestock sent out, of course it was put out on the property. Amy, Aaron, and Mark are charging a small fee to the people who wanted to see the campsite and the buildings on the property, and that fee is for the upkeep of the buildings and ground. Even though we can afford the cost at present time, it could drain us in the long run if we don't charge now.

Several of the men told me that they wanted the stuff to make themselves richer, and it did work for many of them. With some of them it backfired; they couldn't forget what they did, and they were glad when I caught up to them. Some of the men turned themselves in after they heard that I had survived and was on the hunt, and each of them went to jail and was sentenced to hang. All but one was hung and that man died of a heart attack before his execution date. They wanted to be rich, but it brought death to all. They killed all to keep the people from testifying against them. None of them knew that I survived, nor did any of them know that there were other members of the family until it came out in the papers across the country. A second article that appeared on the fifth anniversary telling about my hunting them down brought fear to them, and they shot at everything that moved wrong, sometimes killing their best friends, sometimes innocent people, and sometimes animals. The hunt is over now, and I wish that, that terrible day had never come, and my family would still be alive, but I have learned to trust God in all things, even to the hunting of those men.

Also, while I was talking to many of the men, they told me where each of them were from. Five men came from England; one of them because he had to or go to prison, and another was the sixth son to the second cousin of the king. The other three because they wanted freedom from heavy taxes, and these three are first cousins. Later they went back to claim some property that each of their fathers had left to them. These five met on the ship that brought them over.

Three came from Germany and four men came from Ireland. One came from Spain and three came down from Canada. There were also three Mexicans, two Russians, one from Scotland, one from Poland, three from Italy, four from Austria, one from Egypt, two from Denmark, and one from Cuba. This made a total of thirty-four from foreign countries, many of them still with an accent, so people would know they were not from America. The other one hundred and sixty-six men were born and raised here in America, some from every part of the compass.

April 10, 1893

Today we heard that Buffalo Bill Cody will be at the Chicago World's Fair which will open on May 1. We know that it might be expensive to go up there to see it, but we will do so anyway. We want to get away from here for a few weeks. We will go up by train from here to Chicago and stay there for a couple of weeks.

May 5, 1893

We have been here for three days now. The night before last and last night, we watched Buffalo Bill's Wild West Show and its many acts, and it was fabulous. Today we went back and saw the sideshows. While we were watching some of the sideshows, Buffalo Bill spotted me and came over and asked me if I would join him onstage for one or two shows. I said yes to at least one, and I will work out just what I will do in the show. Later that evening, I performed in the show. I did a few trick shots like Annie Oakley does, but with a twist. I shot with a fast draw to demonstrate what I did when I had to shoot some man who had come at me to kill me, either to finish the job or because I had killed one of his family members.

May 24, 1893

Back home in Colorado, we had another barn dance last night, just like the one on Friday night so many years ago. I saw and danced with Robert, but I only danced two dances with him because he was with his wife, and they danced most of the dances together. They have been happily married for fifteen years now. I was happy for him, for he is not alone anymore. He also has two fine girls; the oldest is named Rebecca, Becky at his wife's insistence because she knew how close we were at one time.

In all the years of travel, I would occasionally stay in the home of someone. Sometimes while there, I would sometimes see something that looked like an item that a family member had before their deaths. If the people could prove they had that piece long before the attack, I would leave it alone. But if the item proved to be one of ours, I would take it back.

Amy is twenty-five, almost twenty-six years old. The year is 1894. My search has been over for three years, and all the men are dead now. I arrived home just before Amy's twenty-third birthday. The last man died a year ago in a Virginia City jail cell. I am still tired, not completely rested from my ordeal. I wake up in the middle of the night sometimes from a bad dream where I am hunting down one of the men and instead of him getting killed, it is I who gets killed. When I wake up, it takes me several minutes to realize that it was only a dream, but by then my sleep has been interrupted. I never wanted to continue the search for that long of a time, but someone had to; they had to pay for what they had done.

Only once in the twenty-two years of the search did we have to charge for supplies and pay for them later. It was when Kate and I rode through Seattle, Washington in late 1886 when we were on our way back from Alaska the second time (the first time was in 1877). When we left Alaska, we knew we had enough money so that we could make it back to Silverton, but as it turned out, just before we reached Seattle, we were robbed and had to walk into town. Fortunately, the people remembered us from the first time through and knew we could be trusted. I am glad that, that was the only time we had to charge. We later heard that the men who robbed us were captured and sent to jail for robbery. Only they said they didn't know who they were robbing, or they would not have done it. They thought they were robbing just a couple of women.

February 8, 1901

In yesterday's *Sagebrush Weekly*, there was a two-column article about Queen Victoria, her life and death. It said that she was born on May 24, 1819, in Kensington, London, England. She was the only daughter of Prince Edward, Duke of Kent and Strathearn, who was the fourth son of George III. She succeeded William IV on June 20, 1837. She married Prince Albert who died in 1861 of typhoid fever. Together they had nine children, five girls and four boys. She passed away on January 22, 1901, on Osborne, Isle of Wight, off the coast of England, after a reign of sixty-three years, seven months, and two days. She is succeeded to the throne by her son, Prince Edward VII.

August 15, 1905

Today I am fifty-five. I was nineteen when I started the search and forty-one when the search was finally over. Kate died on my fifty-second birthday, which was eleven years after the search ended. The following spring, Dawn's mother died, and that fall her aunt died, so she came out to live with me. I am glad to say that Amy never did hate me for leaving her in Uncle Mark's care. In fact, she was a big encouragement to me during those years that I spent away from her, hunting those men down. Even though I was not there with her every day of her growing-up years, she knew why I wasn't there, and she knew that I loved her.

Now I am home to stay, never more to search for the men responsible and to maybe kill them. That was a job I never would have taken if there was another way to make them pay. If some of the men had survived, then maybe they could have done it instead of me. I can now be with Amy and watch my grandchildren grow up, which is what I missed with Amy.

So far, I have seen the invention of both the telephone and the automobile in the 1880s and 1890s, until they were both spread across the United States. I also lived to see my first granddaughter. She was born on my fifty-third birthday which is the year 1903. She was named Rebecca after me. She said that she wanted to keep the name alive in our family for years to come.

Not only did I see all the inventions that came about along with my grandchildren, but the birth of twin great-grandchildren. On May 20, 1928, my granddaughter Becky gave birth to twins, a boy and a girl. She named them Amy Lou and Aaron Andrew, after the only other survivors of the attack.

August 20, 1928

My name is Rebecca Becky Gibson, the granddaughter of Rebecca Sage who had hunted all those men. Five days ago, she was spending the day in town with all of her family to celebrate her seventy-eighth birthday. At about one o'clock, she was standing across the street with all of us including Dawn. At that same moment, a bank robbery was taking place. Something happened inside the bank that made one of the robbers fire his gun. The bullet went out through the glass and found grandma's heart; she never knew what hit her. She was buried yesterday beside her late husband, my grandfather. A very nice headstone was there that she had carved a few years ago, with the words, *Together again at last.*

THE END

ABOUT THE AUTHOR

Christian Smythe was born on August 15, 1950 in Lodi, California. She grew up around Lodi and Galt. She graduated from Galt High in 1970 and joined the army when it was still called Women's Army Corps, WAC for short. She received basic and advanced individual training at Fort McClellan, Alabama. Later, she was transferred to Fort Bragg, North Carolina. There she met and married her husband, and her daughter was born.

They lived in a suburb of Fayetteville, North Carolina. Later she moved back to her hometown.